Heart

OF A

Dove

Also By Abbie Williams

 The Shore Leave Cafe Series

Summer at the Shore Leave Cafe

Second Chances

A Notion of Love

Winter at the White Oaks Lodge

Wild Flower

The First Law of Love

Until Tomorrow

The Way Back

Forbidden

 The Dove Series

Heart of a Dove

Soul of a Crow

Heart

OF A

Dove

Abbie Williams

central
avenue
publishing
2014

CENTRAL AVENUE PUBLISHING EDITION

www.centralavenuepublishing.com

Published in Canada. Printed in the United States of America

First print edition published by Central Avenue Publishing,
an imprint of Central Avenue Marketing Ltd.

HEART OF A DOVE

ISBN 978-1-77168-014-1 (pbk)
ISBN 978-1-77168-015-8 (ebk)

1. FICTION / Romance - Historical   2. FICTION / Historical

This is a work of fiction. Names, characters, places and incidents either are the product of the author's imagination or are used fictitiously and any resemblance to actual persons, living or dead, business establishments, events or locales is entirely coincidental.

Cover Design: Michelle Halket

Cover Images: Courtesy & Copyright shutterstock: Oleg Gekman | PhotoXpress: Hector Fernandez

THIS ONE IS FOR MY DEARS...

D ECORUM. OF ALL the lessons my mother imparted upon me, of
all the ways she attempted to educate me, from the spiritual to the
practical, to classical history and a Shakespearean sonnet or two, this is the
word that flashes into my mind when I think of her. This word in a vivid
slice of memory. Still I am able to hear her low, melodic voice with its hint of
Charleston society, of which nearly two decades in rural Tennessee was never
quite able to rob her.

"Synonyms, Lorissa," she reminded and I chewed my thumbnail in con-
centration before Mama's right eyebrow lifted just a fraction. Immediately
I resettled my hands onto my lap, my shoulders squaring. How I hated the
summer lessons Mama prepared so diligently. I longed to be out under the
sun, with my brothers.

"Decorum," I recited clearly and dutifully. "Synonyms include: modesty,
restraint, respectability, correctness, etiquette, demureness."

"Good behavior," Mama declared to conclude, beaming at me. Her eyes
were green as the stalks of Kentucky bluegrass in full splendor outside our
home. "Well done."

When my heart aches enough that I am unable to bear it, when the mem-
ories of my old life come crackling up beneath the ash pile under which I
deeply buried them years ago, a flame that refuses total annihilation despite
my most agonized effort, this is the vignette that I allow myself to recall:

Afternoon drifting in a lazy fashion towards evening, the long-slanting
sunbeams of late spring bisecting the yard outside the wide, gleaming front
windows. My two older brothers were hanging on the fence, watching as my

father rode his newest acquisition, a lovely blood-bay mare, in a controlled walk around the inner rim of the corral.

In our parlor, Mama closed the copy of *Roget's Thesaurus* she had been using for my lesson and her eyes followed the direction of mine; I was gazing with ill-disguised envy at the activity outside. She allowed, "Enough for today. Why don't you join them?"

I bounded to my feet at once. Mama called after me, "Don't scamper, Lorissa!" but the screen door clacked behind me as I dashed to the corral and climbed up three beams, enough to allow my forearms to line the top-most board, just like the men. Not for the first time I wished I was a boy.

"She's a beauty," murmured my brother Dalton, his elbows hooked over the fence, wide-brimmed hat settled low over his eyes, reminiscent of our father. Dalton was the eldest at sixteen.

"Daddy said she'll be mine," Jesse, a year younger, added. His tone was tinged with awe. I worshiped my brothers, who were lean and lanky and had a bond between them over which I was unfailingly jealous. Both of them had Daddy's curly auburn hair and his eyes, tinted the blue of the gentian salvia that grew in profusion amongst the flower beds on the south side of our house.

"What will you name her?" I asked him, watching as our father halted the mare with a controlled tug. With practiced motions, he shifted his hips and knees, using both hands on the reins, and she lifted her hooves with grace, quick-stepping in a tight circle before resuming her brisk walk in the opposite direction. Our father knew more about horses than anyone in Cumberland County. Likely the entire state of Tennessee.

"I want to ride her before I decide," Jesse said, not removing his reverent eyes from the mare. Her mane and long, proud tail were ebony, as were the bottom joints of her high-stepping legs. The rest of her hide gleamed rust-red in the dying day's sunlight. She tossed her head with a snort as our father came near, halting just before the three of us on the fence.

"What's your opinion, darlin'?" my father asked, peering at me from beneath his gray hat, low-crowned and wide-brimmed, as he favored.

"She's lovely, Daddy," I said. "I wish she was to be mine."

My father laughed, releasing the leather straps in his gloved hands to lift his hat and run the back of one wrist over his forehead.

"When you're fourteen, Lorie," he promised again. "Just like your brothers."

"I know, Daddy," I responded at once.

How could he have known that by my fourteenth birthday he would be dead, killed in far-off Virginia during the battle of Cold Harbor? Both Dalton and Jesse would be long dead by then too, slain at Sharpsburg, like so many of our fellow Tennesseans.

Decorum.

What would my mother have to say if I could hear her voice today? If from some heavenly plane she had the ability to peer downward upon the earth she'd left behind, into the little room that was mine in my seventeenth year? She had wanted so much for me to be a lady. It pained me almost more to imagine my father possessing the same power, able to see what his daughter, his Lorie, had become. Some nights over two dozen men jerked their hips over mine and spilled their seed within my body. Men from all walks of life, but men just the same, with one desire in mind.

I imagined the thesaurus open over my mother's lap, her extended index finger skimming over the page until she found a suitable word.

"Survival, Lorissa," she'd direct.

And dutifully I'd respond, "Survival. Synonyms include: endurance, continued existence, outlasting, subsisting."

"Carrying on," she would say to conclude, her clear green eyes with the expression of tenderness that becomes almost tangible in my memory. As though tenderness is an entity around which I can curl my fingers and cling, never to let go, rather than a heart-wrenching abstraction that tortures me if I'm not on guard.

Occasionally a man caresses my cheek, kisses me as though I mean something more than an average of seven minutes' worth of gold dust from the pouch anchored to his trousers. I am often told I am beautiful; I hear the words 'I love you' more than once a night, to be truthful. I long ago learned that it is common for men to utter this phrase during the act, eyes tightly closed, though it's anyone's guess to whom they are actually referring. Certainly not a prostitute who calls herself Lila.

Ginny forced me to change my name upon entering into her employ. I had been three months into my fifteenth year, no longer cloaked in the numbness of disbelief, though still entrenched in horror and stupefied shock at the death of my mother and subsequently the last living member of my family. Mama had succumbed to fever and chills two days past my birthday, in July of 1865, leaving me utterly alone. Our ranch hands had long since vanished, most to make a stand for the Confederacy, our proud corrals and stables empty but for the aging mare that drew our buggy into town. There was, quite literally, no one left.

Was that an excuse? God knew I often tortured myself in the early morning hours with that very question, after my final customer of the night had donned his clothes and exited my room. Just one day after Mama's death, a neighboring family, the Judsons, had assisted me with her burial. And so began the time during which I was cast about like a bad penny. Mrs. Judson, a sharp-eyed woman with seven of her own children, assured me that I was welcome in their home until arrangements could be made; I had no idea to what arrangements she was referring, near ill with loss and terror and the depths of my aloneness. I remained in their home for a fortnight. Near to August, Mrs. Judson informed me that I would be joining her brother and his wife, along with their three children, as they ventured northwest on a journey to join his wife's family in St. Louis, Missouri. Her brother's wife was sickly, she said, and needed the help.

For weeks, I accompanied Mrs. Judson's brother and his family, the Fosters, in their canvas-topped wagon as it rolled northwest. Mrs. Foster, Annelle had been her name, was kind to me, and I assisted her daily and nightly caring for the children, who ranged in age from five years to four months. Mr. Foster preferred to disregard my presence when his wife was near, though I felt a twisting in my gut at the way his eyes followed me intently when she was not. Mrs. Foster, who spit blood into her countless linen handkerchiefs, died before we'd reached our destination, only miles from St. Louis. Mr. Foster managed to bury her and subsequently get us into town before determining my fate. I'd been sick with unease at what Mr. Foster would choose to do with me; it turned out he struck a deal without my knowledge, after a night of drinking and gambling while I waited in the wagon with his children.

And that was how, in October of 1865, a fifteen year old girl once named Lorissa became an employee at Ginny Hossiter's whore house.

G ODDAMMIT, I TOLD you I didn't have time to show her around," grumbled the woman who had been roused from her bed, though it was well past the noon hour. She wore a rose-pink robe with gold embroidery, though it was frayed at the hem and belted loosely over her naked body. Her breasts wobbled beneath, unrestrained by any corset, and her legs were bare from the knee down. I was so shocked I hardly knew where to let my eyes rest. She looked at me with undiluted annoyance, lips cinched up like the drawstrings of a purse, and demanded, "Girl, what's your name?"

I opened my mouth to speak but found that I could not force a sound past the lump of fear. As her eyes narrowed, I cleared my throat in a hurry and responded, "Lorissa, ma'am."

"Oh, 'ma'am' is it?" And then she laughed deep in her throat, leaning back.

The man who had escorted me up the staircase spoke with sharp impatience, saying, "Ginny wants her acquainted with the place, Jola. That's what she told me, and you been here longest."

The woman named Jola shuddered lightly and said, "Don't remind me. Jesus, how did I get so lucky? Well, come on, girl, let's show you around the place."

The man sighed with palpable relief and I watched his back bounce as he descended the stairs to the ground level, before I let my eyes move cautiously back to the woman. Jola studied at me a bit more closely then, her eyes censuring. I held in a frightened breath and forced myself to remain still as her gaze swept over me from hat to hemline. She said, "Ginny'll get her money's worth with you, girl. You're a lovely little thing. How'd you end up here? Where's your family?"

Too many questions for my muddled mind; I managed, "Passed, ma'am," and then she nodded in a knowing fashion.

"So many have," she said, and I sensed that was as near to empathy as she would manage. "How old are you?"

"Fifteen," I whispered. Terror rose swiftly in my chest, and the sharp edges of sobs, but I sensed deeply I could not allow myself to lose composure.

"Same age as I was when I started here," she said. And then, "You been with a man? You haven't the look of it about you."

I shook my head. My heart was thrusting so violently that I was certain that I may very well die at her feet, here in the upper hallway of this place. Her mouth drew in again, as though she was attempting to pick up an apple seed with her lips. She tightened the belt on her robe and said, "Well, never mind that now. Come along, I'll show you to your room."

She led me past three closed doors to a miniscule room on the left side of the hall, where the door gaped open. I followed, clutching my valise. The space was dominated by a stripped bed, brass-framed, with ornate designs of roses on the posts. There was a small chest of drawers topped by an oval mirror in a wooden frame, a straight-backed chair, a dressing screen painted with peacocks, a coat rack, nothing more. No carpet to warm the bare plank floor. A single window faced west and allowed a splash of sunlight to spill across the bed; gauzy white curtains were drawn to the bustle of the day outside.

"Betsy will get this made for you directly," Jola said, indicating the bed. "And I'm supposing you haven't a thing suitable to wear. Well, the girls will have to outfit you." She stepped closer, reached and touched my hair with familiarity, again prompting my desire to cringe away. But I stood still and allowed her touch. She smoothed a strand back into my braid, trailing her fingertips over my chin, turning me to face the light. "You're angel-faced, girl. The men'll be fighting over you. Where you'd get eyes so blue-green?"

Footsteps were clicking down the hall, authoritatively. Moments later Ginny Hossiter was framed in the doorway, dressed in a full-skirted gown of emerald satin, with paste-brilliants decorating the bodice and emphasizing her considerable cleavage. Her dark hair was arranged into a coronet atop her head, further adorned with brilliants and a single peacock feather. I would not have been able to accurately guess her age; she could have been anywhere between thirty and fifty, so heavily made-up that it was impossible to discern.

As they had when I was first introduced to her scarce a half hour past, her dark eyes caused my stomach to ache with fear.

She said, "This will be your room from now on." And then, again shocking me, though I should have been well beyond feeling so by now, "When did you last bleed, girl?"

I gulped, palms sweaty on the handle of my valise. I thought back desperately and then said, "Two weeks past, ma'am."

Jola laughed, dropping her hands from my face. She muttered, "'Ma'am' it is then. I could get used to that."

"Shut your mouth," Ginny snapped and Jola did so, but sullenly. Jola was perhaps ten years older than me and had likely once been quite pretty; though now her face was pinched somehow, her eyes hard as flint. Ginny went on, "Good, that's perfect timing. What is your name? I don't recall."

My vision slicked to a pinpoint, making me want to reel forward. With effort I remained upright and said, "Lorissa Blake, ma'am."

Ginny raked her eyes over me and then said decisively, "Your name will be Lila, as of today. That's a proper name for a whore, and it suits you. You've a face that will make me money." She smoothed her hands over the satin belly of her gown and then swished into the room, taking me by the elbow and turning me in a slow circle. "I was assured of your virginity, is that right?" Her eyes dared me to contradict this question.

"That's right," I whispered, my throat tight. I felt as though a giant fist was closing slowly over my windpipe and, not for the first time since Mama's death, longed for my own. How would I possibly do what would be demanded here of me? I would likely die anyway, from the shame and horror.

"That'll fetch a proper pot of gold," she said, and her lips slid back over her teeth in what I knew was meant to be a smile. Growing quite businesslike, she added, "You are entitled to a percentage of everything you earn for me. I don't expect service for nothing, you know. You'll be allowed three meals a day, laundry, bathing. My house is clean, my girls are clean. I won't stand for otherwise. I don't stand for the Frenchy sex here, either. Men can go elsewhere for that sort of thing. Otherwise you do exactly what they want, you understand? Most of them men don't last long, isn't that right, Jola?"

Jola nodded in affirmation, picking at something in her front teeth. She contributed, "And most are so happy to be getting their peckers soaked they won't mistreat you, Lila. And Horace is here if anyone turns ugly on you. Don't happen often, though."

I nodded. My chest was aching, as though I'd been dealt a severe blow there.

"When you bleed, you get them days free," Jola continued. "We all take our turns. When you bleed, you're in charge of hanging out laundry. Betsy will leave the butter douche for you to use every morning otherwise."

"The what?" I faltered, stomach lurching, and I was certain that if Jim Foster were before me in this moment, and I was fortunate enough to possess a sharp knife, I would sink its entire length into his right eye, with no regrets. Never before had such a violent notion crossed my mind.

"It's how we avoid getting caught," Jola said impatiently. "Ain't none of us wants a child, believe me. After each trick, you squat over the bowl and use your fingers to clean yourself out. Got a mixture of potash salts and vinegar in the butter, cleans out their seeds right quick."

Please, God, take me from here. Mama, oh God, Mama, help me.

Somehow, even then, I sensed no prayers were answered here. Again I could only nod, weakly.

Ginny flicked her skirts and addressed Jola. "You see that she gets outfitted today. I want her looking like a doll tonight. Damnation, it's Saturday and we'll draw a crowd with our new peach." Her eyes came back to me and she added, "We'll make them bid for you, doll."

And she disappeared.

Jola joined me on the mattress and affected an air of concern as she said, "Don't worry, honey, you'll be all right. It takes some time. But you'll get the hang of it." She looked up then, as a new figure appeared in the doorway. "Afternoon, Deirdre, this here is Lila, Ginny's new girl."

The new woman stepped into the room and considered me. She too was clad in a dressing gown, though hers was a creamy yellow, with blue forget-me-nots trailing over its length. She was winsome, pale as milk and certainly younger than Jola, with long black hair and eyes as big as a doe's in a narrow white face. She said, "Pleased to meet you, Lila."

I sensed kindness in her voice, a softness. She joined us, sitting on my other side and reaching to feel my hair, as Jola had done. Though her hands were gentle rather than speculative.

"Jola, a moment?" she asked.

Deirdre rose gracefully, as Jola disappeared down the hall, and eased my door nearly closed. I watched her silently. When she took her place again on the bed, she said, "You're just a girl. I heard what Ginny was saying about making them bid for you. Damn her. She's got the devil in her, Lila, believe me."

When I didn't speak, she continued, taking my cold hands into hers, "It's not an easy thing to get used to, but it won't hurt after the first few times, I promise. Do you know anything about a man's body?" She studied my eyes and concluded, "No, you don't. Where did you come from?"

"Lafayette, Tennessee," I whispered. "My daddy owned a ranch there. He was killed in the War."

"My husband, too," she whispered, and her eyes closed for a moment. When she opened them, she said, "Men are all the same when it comes to rutting, Lila. It's what drives them. I learned about men from my Joshua, but I did love him. We were married but a year before he was killed. I've had too many men to count by now, but I still remember the sweetness of what we had then. It can be a blessed thing, but here you won't find that." She tipped her head to the side and asked, "Have you seen horses mate, perhaps? You said a ranch…"

I nodded at that, cringing at the thought of the arm-sized phallus of a horse.

"Well, a man's pecker gets rigid like a horse's, though not near the size," and she giggled before going on, "And all they want to do when it gets rigid is stick it up inside the nearest woman they can find. Right here," she said, indicating her lap. "Within you, where a baby would be birthed. It does ache the first time, and you'll bleed, there's no helping that. But butter helps ease their passage, if you're too sore."

My stomach rolled, in pure horror.

"And they'll move it in and out, faster and faster, usually, until their pecker bursts. That's what you must clean out in the mornings, that's what will lead to a child. Some may want to kiss you, or suckle your breasts, but most just want their time inside of you. Most don't take the time to pretend affection." Deirdre looked at me in sympathy. "You'll learn." And then, "Have you any gowns to wear?"

At the last moment I turned, blindly. Deirdre understood and scrambled for the basin under the bed, getting it to my chin as I heaved. There was blessed little in my stomach, hardly enough to cause alarm, but I could not stop retching, gasping for breaths in between each. Deirdre held the basin until I calmed a measure, curling around my stomach on the bare mattress. I wanted to be dead, and yet I was too afraid to take my own life, for fear of retribution. My only hope was that I would be reunited with my family in heaven, someday. If I took my own life, I would not be allowed that privilege.

"You must get ahold of yourself," Deirdre scolded, but kindly. "You must, Lila. There is no other choice, not here. And you mark my words about Ginny. It doesn't do to anger her."

I remembered well how Mama would laugh as she'd say, *"Speak of the devil and he shall appear!"* usually in reference to one of my brothers. Those words burned in my mind just then, as clicking footsteps sounded.

"Sit up, quick!" Deirdre demanded, whisking the basin out of sight.

I did as she bade just as Ginny sailed through the door, her arms burdened with garments. These she flung onto the chair alongside the bed and ordered, "Deirdre, outfit her. I've been spreading the word about our little virgin here, and I want her ready for show in three hours. You hear?" Her dark eyes included me in the question.

"Of course," said Deirdre, in a different tone than she'd been using with me, and I forced myself to nod.

Ginny disappeared yet again.

Jola returned with a tray containing a tea pot, three porcelain cups, scones laced with cream, butter, sliced ham and boiled potatoes. She plunked this upon the bed and nodded to it, suggesting, "You best eat while you can. After the place gets busy you'll be holed up in here 'til morning light."

Deirdre took my hands once again and eased me to my feet, saying, "Let's get you undressed and bathed, first thing. We've a bath off the kitchen. I'll have Betsy start heating water for you."

An hour later I'd been scrubbed and doused unceremoniously by the servant woman named Betsy, with Deirdre overseeing. She kept a running commentary as Betsy worked over me, perhaps to dispel my quaking nerves, but mostly because I needed to know the information she was imparting. Though my blessings were few, I thanked God for Deirdre, who seemed truly kind.

"Betsy, here, won't be available to bathe you every day," she said.